SATOMI ICHIKAWA

Friends

Parents' Magazine Press · New York

Copyright © 1976 by Satomi Ichikawa
Published by Parents' Magazine Press 1977
First published by William Heinemann, Ltd, London
Printed in the United States of America
All rights reserved

Library of Congress Cataloging in Publication Data

Ichikawa, Satomi.
  Friends.

  SUMMARY: Sharing fun, such as playing in the
  park, dressing up to make believe, or having a
  pillow fight, keeps friends together.
  [1. Friendship—Fiction] I. Title.
PZ7.I16Fr   [E]   76-46146
ISBN 0-8193-0870-6   ISBN 0-8193-0871-4 lib. bdg.

Friends, friends, friends
We will always be.
Whether in fair or in dark, stormy weather,
The fun we have will keep us together.

We need friends

to play with,

for jumping over,

and bumping over,

and making mean ugly faces—

or beautiful smiling faces.

We need friends to help draw big pictures...

and sometimes to share the blame.

Sh-h-h. Friends need quiet

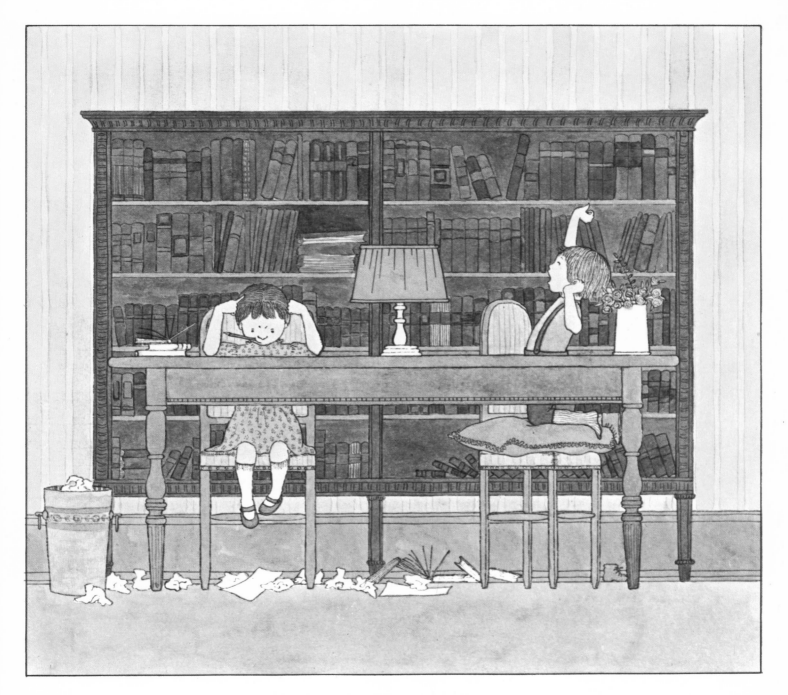

for doing homework together.

A friend will keep a secret

and listen to a silly story.
(Grandpas can be best friends, too.)

A friend will rummage with you,

and play make-believe—

even build a house,

and pretend to live inside.

Friends will bring their old toys to backyard sales...

and won't be angry when accidents happen.

We need friends for cleaning up, and getting dirty—

then cleaning up again,

for blowing bubbles at,

or just watching them float high into the sky.

We need friends to explore meadows,

and discover treasures,

to keep us company when mother is out shopping,

and to make beautiful music with.

Best of all, we need friends for sleep-overs,

and pillow fights, and late goodnights.

We're friends, friends, friends.